Emily and the Snowflake

By Jan Wahl
Illustrated by Carolyn Ewing

WHISTLESTOP

Troll

For Lauren and Elisabeth Sher

This edition published in 2001.
Text copyright © 1995 by Jan Wahl.
Illustrations copyright © 1995 by Carolyn Ewing.
Published by WhistleStop, an imprint and trademark of
Troll Communications L.L.C.

Library of Congress Cataloging-in-Publication Data

Wahl, Jan
Emily and the Snowflake / by Jan Wahl
p.   cm.
Summary: On the day before Christmas, Emily waits for the first snowflake to fall.
ISBN 0-8167-3573-5
(1. Christmas—Fiction.   2. Snow—Fiction.)   I. Title.
PZ7.W1266Em   1995   (E)—dc20   94-22713

It was the morning before Christmas, and no snow had fallen yet.

Emily Rosebush bundled up warm. She gazed at a broad, mysterious sky. The sky seemed to be one huge cloud.

"There *must* be a hole up there," Emily said to herself. "Soon maybe a snowflake will fall and I can catch it."

Inside the house, her mother, Mrs. Rosebush, marched back and forth. She was busy hanging mistletoe and green fir branches.

"Emily, why don't you go outside?" her mother had said. "You just might find the first snowflake."

That was a good idea.

At noon her father returned, carrying a brown box with small holes.

Emily pretended not to see him shift it to his other side. She kept studying the silver sky.

"What are you looking for?" asked Mr. Rosebush.

"The first snowflake," said Emily. "I am Snowflake Keeper Number 1. An important job!" She showed him a small, blue tin box.

"When it falls," she said, "I will catch it in this."
"Ah. Best of luck," replied her father. And he hurried into the house with the brown box.

Everybody was in a crazy hurry on the day before Christmas, wrapping or hiding things.

But Emily stood outside, waiting to do her special job, to catch the first snowflake.

Overhead the sky hung thick as gray wool. At last the very
first snowflake twinkled down.

"Come here!" Emily ordered.

The flake failed to listen. Quickly she bobbed about the
yard. Without a sound, the snowflake landed in her box.

She snapped the lid shut.

Snowflake Keeper Number 1 rushed into the house to show it off. Her father gave an odd cough.

"Oh, we didn't hear you."

Her mother's hand was on the knob to the cellar door. Emily almost didn't notice.

"I have it!" Emily squealed, opening the box. Both parents peeked in.

"A lovely drop of water," said her father.

"Yes, a fine drop," echoed her mother.

"Lock the doors!" wailed Emily. "Someone stole my snowflake!"

At that moment, a howl rose from the cellar. "What's down there?" Emily wanted to know.

"Nothing," said her father. "Maybe the same wind that brought your snowflake."

"I don't have any snowflake," cried Emily.

"Yes you do," said her mother. With a pair of scissors, she cut a snowflake out of white paper and gave it to Emily.

Emily stared at it.

"Wow, what a wonderful, excellent snowflake," she fibbed.

"It will never, ever melt," said her father. And her parents went right back to their secrets.

The rest of that whole long day, Emily carried the paper cutout around in the tin box. But she was sad.

It was not enough to get a snowflake made of paper. She wanted the real thing.

To forget, Emily helped her father bake gingersnap cookies.

Each one was in the shape of a roly-poly snowman. They covered the cookies with icing.

Later she and her mother hung them on the prickly pine tree.

From time to time, she heard a howling from the cellar.

"If that *is* wind," said Emily, "I hope it brings a ton of snow."

However, that night when Emily went to bed, there still was no snow on the ground.

All she had was a paper snowflake.

She heard her parents talking downstairs. She closed her eyes and was soon dreaming.

She met a snowman named Mr. Woggle. He handed her a card with his name printed on it.

She admired his purple mittens. He took her by the hand.

Together both of them walked down to Thelma Smith's
store on Gruber Street. Snow was piled high.
It was amazing how Mr. Woggle could walk without legs.

They sat on green leather stools. Mr. Woggle had a sore throat and did not talk. So Emily ordered.

"Two pistachio cones, please," she said.

Emily was enjoying the cone and company. Then—all at once—her dream drifted off and she awoke.

Sniffing cranberry waffles, Emily quickly got dressed and ran downstairs. Out in the yard she saw dazzling snow.

Presents lay under a beautifully lit tree. "Where do I start?"
she exclaimed.

"Start with the waffles. They are still hot," said Mr. Rosebush.

"Swell idea," said Emily as she sat down at the table. However, before Emily finished eating, she heard a terrific scratching noise and a yipping from under the tree.

All the Rosebushes ran to the living room.
"One of the presents—" said her mother.
"—is alive!" finished her father.

Darting under the tree, Emily opened
the noisy, wrapped box with strange holes.
Inside wiggled a puppy who snuggled
up to her.
"Can you give him a name?" asked
Mr. Rosebush quietly.

"Think hard," said Mrs. Rosebush.
The dog wagged a frisky tail. And he
gave Emily an early Christmas morning kiss.
"Snowflake!" said Emily Rosebush.